D0997017

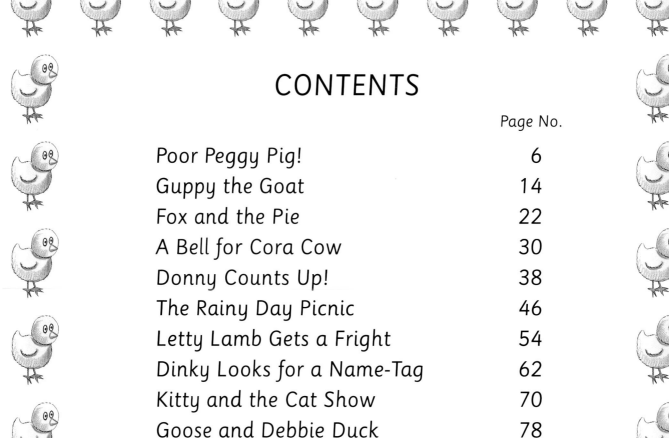

CONTENTS

First Published 2000 by Brown Watson
The Old Mill, 76 Fleckney Road,
Kibworth Beauchamp, Leics LE8 0HG

ISBN: 978-0-7097-1344-9

Reprinted 2001, 2002, 2003, 2004, 2005 (twice), 2006, 2007, 2009

Printed in China

NOW I CAN READ

15
Farm Stories

Stories by Maureen Spurgeon
Illustrations by Stephen Holmes

Brown Watson
ENGLAND

POOR PEGGY PIG!

Poor Peggy Pig! The wind had blown a hole in her sty!

'Oh, dear!' she said. 'I must find a new home!' So she set off.

'I need a new home!' she told Dinky Dog. 'Can I come in your kennel?'

'Sorry,' said Dinky. 'You are MUCH too big!' Poor Peggy Pig!

On she went to the farmhouse.

'Do not bother me, Peggy!' said Cook. 'I must find a lost kitten!'

Poor Peggy Pig! 'I need a new home!' she told Hector Horse.

'Can I come in your stable?'

'No!' said Hector. 'You smell!'

'I smell like all other pigs!' Peggy said. 'YOU smell too!'

'Yes,' said Hector, 'but I smell like other horses!'

Poor Peggy Pig! On and on she went, looking for a new home. It grew dark. Then she saw a door and the glow of two tiny eyes.

How glad Peggy was to go in and lie down! She felt so hot and so very, very tired.

'Peggy!' cried the farmer the next day. 'What HAVE you done? One, two, three...' he counted.

'Four, five, six...' said Dinky.

'Seven, eight, nine,' counted Hector, 'TEN fine piglets!'

'Clever Peggy Pig!' cried the farmer. 'How did you find your way inside this old trailer?'

'MEW!' mewed the kitten.

'Well, well!' said the farmer. 'Now I must make a new sty for you and your ten piglets!' And he did!

Clever Peggy Pig!

READ THESE WORDS AGAIN!

wind	sty
hole	house
kitten	stable
smell	new
two	eyes
tired	mewed
clever	inside

12

WHAT CAN YOU SEE HERE?

pig

kennel

farmer

piglet

horse

13

GUPPY THE GOAT

'What use is Guppy Goat?' said Hector Horse. 'What does he do?'

'He does not give milk,' said Cora Cow.

'He does not lay eggs,' said Hetty Hen.

'He is useless!' said Hector.

'Guppy IS nice!' said Donny Donkey. But nobody listened.

'They say I am useless!' Guppy told Kitten. 'All except Donny!'

'They do not mean it!' said Kitten. 'Cheer up, Guppy!'

Just then, Guppy saw that a gate had been left open. He bent down and slipped one horn under the latch. Then he pushed the gate shut and let the latch fall.

Next, he saw some paper on the ground. He used his horns to pick up the paper and put the bits in a bin. He stuck one horn into a tin can which had been thrown into a tree. That went into the bin, too.

Then, some boys began chasing sheep! How Guppy chased those boys away!

The sheep bleated in fright. One got caught on a wire fence. But Guppy nibbled and chewed at the sheep's wool until it was free.

'Thank you, Guppy!' said the farmer. 'Kitten said you closed the gate, you picked up all the litter and you chased those boys away! Now you have saved a sheep! You work so hard on our farm!'

And when they heard all that Guppy had done, the other animals had to agree! Clever old Guppy!

READ THESE WORDS AGAIN!

what	useless
listened	except
cheer	slipped
horn	pushed
ground	saved
work	hard
other	agree

WHAT CAN YOU SEE HERE?

gate

latch

Guppy
Goat

litter

boys

FOX AND THE PIE

One day, a fox crept into the farm.
'Go away!' barked Dinky Dog.

'Now, now!' purred Fox. 'I have only come to see you!'

'And to steal food!' said Dinky. She barked again.

The farmer's wife came out. 'Fox!' she cried, but Fox was already across the yard!

Soon, Fox saw Guppy Goat next to the wall. In his mouth was a big, tasty-looking pie, left over from a picnic.

'Hello, Guppy!' said Fox. 'My, what a tasty-looking pie!'

'Yes..' began Guppy. As he opened his mouth, out fell the pie! Fox snapped it up and ran off. What a feast for a hungry fox!

Along came Donny Donkey. 'Fox!' he brayed. 'What a tasty-looking pie!'

Fox nodded his head. He was smarter than Guppy!

'I saw another fox with a pie like that,' said Donny. 'But his was MUCH bigger!' Fox nearly opened his mouth in surprise! Donny led him to a stream.

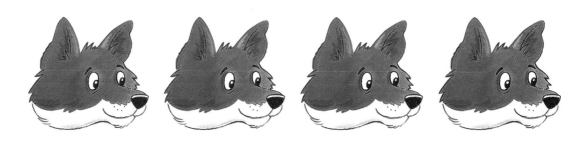

'There he is!' said Donny. He nodded at the water. 'See that pie!'

Fox looked into the stream. Looking up at him was another fox with a big pie in his mouth!

Fox gave a growl. SPLASH! His pie fell into the stream. Fox growled again, this time with rage!

'Still up to your tricks, Fox?' shouted the farmer's wife, and she chased him away with a broom.

And the pie? By the time Donny fished it out, it was already soggy, but it was just as tasty as it looked!

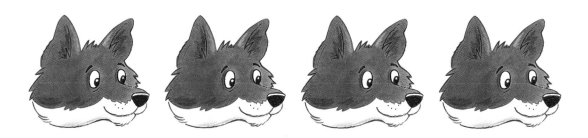

READ THESE WORDS AGAIN!

crept	barked
steal	purred
yard	mouth
snapped	opened
surprise	growl
splash	rage
already	soggy

WHAT CAN YOU SEE HERE?

fox

tasty-looking pie

stream

wall

broom

A BELL FOR CORA COW

Cora Cow won a gold bell at a show! 'I shall wear it on a ribbon all the time!' she said.

'You must take it off when you eat,' said Dinky Dog.

'And when you sleep!' said Pixie Puppy.

'Then I may lose it!' said Cora. 'No! I shall not take it off!'

Cora went to the meadow, the bell tinkling and jingling. She sat in the shade of a tree and closed her eyes. The bell tinkled. She moved her head.

The bell jingled. She stood up. The bell tinkled. 'I shall go to the stream and have a drink!' she said.

At the stream she bent her head towards the cool water. The bell slipped down in front of her face, tinkling and jingling. Whatever she did, the bell got in the way.

So, Cora went to find some grass to eat, the bell still tinkling. She bent down. The bell tinkled and jingled. She tried moving her head. But, she could not move!

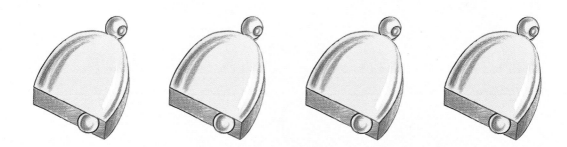

'Moo!' cried Cora, her bell tinkling even louder. 'Help me!'

'Your ribbon has caught on the bush!' said the farmer. 'I will cut you free with my scissors!'

Cora said nothing. Her poor neck felt so stiff and sore.

'Your bell is a bit dented,' said the farmer. 'But it still jingles. Shall we hang it up in the cow shed?' Cora nodded. How nice it was not to have the tinkling and jingling of the bell around her neck!

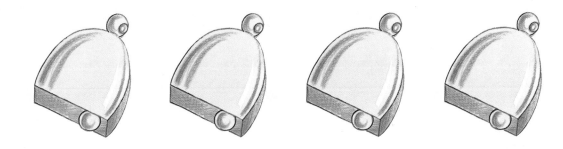

READ THESE WORDS AGAIN!

gold   tinkling

jingling   shade

moved   head

front   face

whatever   find

some   tried

caught   stiff

WHAT CAN YOU SEE HERE?

bell

ribbon

tree

grass

scissors

DONNY COUNTS UP!

There was going to be a birthday party for Pixie Puppy!

'Carrots for Hector Horse!' said Dinky Dog, emptying a sack. 'Corn for Hetty Hen. Bran for Peggy Pig. How many dishes do we need, Donny Donkey?'

'Hetty Hen, one,' began Donny. 'Hector Horse, two. Billy Goat, three. Guppy Goat, four. Kitty Cat, five. Cora Cow, six. Peggy Pig, seven. And you, Dinky! Eight!'

'No!' said Dinky. 'Count again!'

So Donny counted. 'Hetty Hen, one. Hector Horse, two. Billy Goat, three. Guppy Goat, four. Kitty Cat, five. Cora Cow, six. Peggy Pig, seven. Dinky, eight and – I forgot Pixie! Nine!'

'Is that right?' asked Dinky.

'Yes!' cried Donny. 'That IS right!'

'Right!' said Dinky. 'You can put the dishes out!' So Donny began.

'Hetty Hen, one. Hector Horse, two. Billy Goat, three. Guppy Goat, four. Kitty Cat, five. Cora Cow, six. Peggy Pig, seven. Dinky, eight. Pixie, nine.'

Donny stopped. 'What about ME?' he said.

'You forgot to count yourself!' said Dinky. 'NOW count again!'

So Donny counted. 'Hetty Hen, one. Hector Horse, two. Billy Goat, three. Guppy Goat, four. Kitty cat, five. Cora Cow, six. Peggy Pig, seven. Dinky, eight. Pixie, nine, and ME, makes TEN!'

'Right!' said Donny. 'Now let us go and find the others and Pixie Puppy can have a LOVELY birthday party!'

READ THESE WORDS AGAIN!

birthday   party

carrots   emptying

dishes   one

two   count

again   forgot

right   eight

puppy   lovely

WHO CAN YOU SEE HERE?

Dinky Dog

Hetty Hen

Donny Donkey

Guppy Goat

Pixie Puppy

THE RAINY DAY PICNIC

It was a warm, sunny day. The animals were going on a picnic! There were apples for Peggy Pig, corn for Hetty Hen, carrots for Donny Donkey, hay for Hector Horse, biscuits for Dinky Dog and Pixie Puppy – and lots of other food to share.

Only Guppy Goat had seen a big, black cloud in the sky. The animals had just reached the woods, when it began to rain.

'Take shelter!' cried Hector Horse.

'Bother the rain!' said Pixie Puppy.
'This picnic was going to be fun!'

Just then they heard splashing.

'Summer rain is nice and warm!'
quacked Debbie Duck.

'We like getting wet!' added Drake.
'So do the ducklings!'

The ducks looked so happy that
Peggy Pig was soon rolling about in
mud! 'Bathe those big feet of yours,
Hector Horse!' she grunted.

'Let us jump in the puddles!' cried
Donny Donkey.

Dinky began splashing about.

Pixie paddled in the puddles!

They were having such fun in the rain, nobody had seen the sun coming out!

'Look!' cried Donny. 'A rainbow! That is made by the sun shining on raindrops!'

They looked up at the rainbow. The rain had made the woods smell so fresh, and it had kept the picnic food nice and cool.

'I think,' said Guppy Goat, between bites of a crusty roll, 'this is the best picnic we have ever had!'

READ THESE WORDS AGAIN!

sunny	picnic
apples	carrots
reached	rain
shelter	bother
splashing	ducklings
grunted	bathe
jump	raindrops

WHAT CAN YOU SEE HERE?

apples

biscuits

rainbow

puddles

black cloud

LETTY LAMB GETS A FRIGHT

Letty Lamb was always frightened! 'Baa!' she went as a leaf rustled. 'That frightened me. Baa!' she bleated at Kitten. 'You DID give me a fright!'

'No need to get frightened!' said Dinky Dog. But it was no use.

One hot afternoon, there was a distant rumble of thunder.

'Baa!' cried Letty. 'A storm! Storms frighten me! I must hide!'

Letty was frightened and ran inside an old barn.

Outside, the lightning flashed and thunder crashed overhead.

'BAA!' said Letty as loud as she could. 'BAA! Help! Help!'

There was a loud CRACK and then a CRASH! A big hole appeared in the roof. She could see the lightning flashing. The thunder got louder.

'Baa!' she bleated. 'Baa! BAA!'

'We are coming, Letty!' came the farmer's voice. 'A tree has crashed through the roof!'

The farmer and another man came inside the barn.

'Quick!' said the farmer. 'Cover all this hay to keep it dry! It is the winter feed for the animals!'

'Good thing we got here before it all got soaked!' said the man.

'Yes!' said the farmer. 'Thanks to brave Letty Lamb! She stayed here, bleating, until help came!'

'BAA!' said Letty. 'I am so ...' She stopped. Outside, lightning flashed and thunder crashed, but she was not frightened any more!

READ THESE WORDS AGAIN!

frightened	rustled
afternoon	thunder
storm	overhead
louder	crashed
hole	winter
feed	soaked
stayed	help

WHAT CAN YOU SEE HERE?

leaf

lightning

an old barn

roof

hay

DINKY LOOKS FOR A NAME-TAG

'I have lost my name-tag!' cried Dinky Dog. 'It was on my collar!'

'Think,' said Peggy Pig. 'Where do you remember seeing it last?'

'When I went to see Hector Horse!' said Dinky. 'Maybe my name-tag is in the stable!' So she set off.

'I have not seen your name-tag,' said Hector, 'but I found this ribbon belonging to Kitty Cat.'

'I will take it to her,' said Dinky. 'My name-tag could be at the farmhouse!' So, she set off.

Kitty was glad to have her ribbon!
'I have not seen your name-tag, Dinky,' she said, 'but I found this straw hat belonging to Donny Donkey!'

'I will take it to him,' said Dinky. 'My name-tag could be in the cabbage patch!' So, she set off.

Donny was glad to have his straw hat! 'I have not seen your name-tag, Dinky,' he said, 'but I found this bell belonging to Guppy Goat!'

'I will take it to him,' said Dinky. 'My name-tag could be in the meadow!' So, she set off.

Guppy was out in the meadow and was very pleased to see Dinky bringing his bell back.

'Thank you, Dinky,' he said.

'Now go and see Cora Cow, I think she is looking for you.'

Dinky found Cora in the cowshed. She was holding something round and shiny in her mouth and looking very pleased with herself.

'Your name-tag, Dinky! I wanted you to have it back, before you began looking all over the farm!'

READ THESE WORDS AGAIN!

lost	collar
horse	found
ribbon	belonging
house	something
meadow	pleased
looking	bell
shiny	began

WHAT CAN YOU SEE HERE?

cowshed

name-tag

cabbage patch

straw hat

stable

KITTY AND THE CAT SHOW

'Kitty Cat can be in a Cat Show at the Summer Fair!' said the farmer's wife one day.

Dinky Dog was surprised. Kitty was big and fat. Her fur was patchy and one ear was too big – not the sort of cat to be in a Cat Show! He went to tell the other animals.

'Well,' said Hetty Hen, 'Kitty IS a nice cat...'

'And she has a LOVELY purr,' said Donny Donkey.

'But she is not pretty,' said Kitten.

'I think I shall go to the Cat Show, as well!'

'We shall ALL go,' said Donny. 'Just to see what happens!'

At the Summer Fair, there were stalls with prizes to be won. There were roundabouts and swings and lucky dips, balloons and flags for everyone – and a big tent with a poster saying, CAT SHOW.

'Wait!' said Kitten. 'I must make myself look smart!' She smoothed her whiskers, washed her fur and cleaned her paws. Then they went inside.

They soon saw Kitty! She had just won a cup for being the cat with the loudest purr! Hetty, Dinky and Donny were pleased. Kitten tried to get a closer look.

'What a pretty kitten!' said a man with a camera. 'I must take her picture for my newspaper!'

Well! That made everyone VERY pleased. And Kitten? She was so happy, her purr was nearly as loud as Kitty's!

READ THESE WORDS AGAIN!

summer	fair
patchy	fur
pretty	lovely
purr	poster
whiskers	smoothed
loudest	nearly
happy	pleased

WHAT CAN YOU SEE HERE?

Kitty Cat

camera

Kitten

newspaper

balloons

GOOSE AND DEBBIE DUCK

Goose and Debbie Duck were always quarrelling!

'Your ducklings kept me awake!'

'They did not!'

'Yes they did!'

In the end, they did not talk at all. So all was quiet when poachers came to steal from the farm. They crept up on Debbie and her ducklings, meaning to steal the biggest one.

Then – HONK! HONK! Goose appeared. Her wings were spread wide and she was hissing loudly.

She pecked at the men and they began shouting.

'See those poachers off my land, Dinky Dog!' cried the farmer. 'They came up against our brave goose!'

Debbie wanted to show she was brave, too! She had an idea! If she took two goose eggs, Goose would think they had been stolen. Then, Debbie could pretend to save them!

Debbie waited for her chance. Then she took two eggs back to her nest.

'Two of my eggs have been taken!' cried Goose. 'My poor goslings!'

But Debbie was too frightened to give the eggs back! Soon, the shells cracked and two tiny heads peeped out, cheeping at Debbie.

'My goslings!' cried Goose. 'You found them, Debbie!'

Now Debbie felt more ashamed than ever, but Mother Goose was too happy to notice.

'Thank you for taking care of them, Debbie!' she said. 'We MUST be friends forever, now!'

And they were. Most of the time.

READ THESE WORDS AGAIN!

quarrelling awake

quiet crept

appeared hissing

pecked brave

idea stolen

two peeped

ashamed notice

WHO CAN YOU SEE HERE?

Goose

ducklings

poachers

goslings

friends

COCKEREL TRIES TO SLEEP

It had been a long, hot day.

'Get a good night's sleep, Cockerel,' said the farmer. 'We need you to wake us early tomorrow!'

Cockerel yawned. He could not sleep until the sun had set! At last, he closed his eyes.

'Ee-Aar!' sounded the alarm on the farmer's car. Cockerel woke up.

'Cock-a-doodle-doo!' he crowed.

'Quiet, Cockerel!' cried the farmer. 'Get a good night's sleep!'

Cockerel had to find a quieter place to sleep! He went to the stream and curled up under a tree.

'Quack!' said Debbie Duck. 'Do not squash my ducklings!'

Cockerel woke up. 'Cock-a-doodle-doo!' he crowed.

'Be quiet, Cockerel!' barked Dinky. 'Get a good night's sleep!'

Cockerel went to find a quieter place to sleep. He crept into the stable and curled up on the hay. A wisp of hay blew past Hector Horse. 'ATISHOO!' he sneezed. Cockerel woke up.

'Cock-a-doodle-doo!' he crowed.

'Quiet, Cockerel!' grunted Peggy Pig. 'Get a good night's sleep!'

Cockerel went to find a quieter place to sleep. He curled up in the farmyard. His eyes were just closing, when the sun began to rise.

'Cock-a-doodle-doo!' he crowed. Everybody woke up.

'What a terrible night!' said the farmer. 'Cockerel kept us awake!'

'Yes!' said Dinky. 'And you told him to get a good night's sleep!'

READ THESE WORDS AGAIN!

wake	sleep
early	tomorrow
yawned	sounded
alarm	quieter
crowed	wisp
sneezed	curled
closing	kept

WHAT CAN YOU SEE HERE?

cockerel

night

farmyard

tree

sun

DONNY AND SAMMY SCARECROW

Donny Donkey never went far away from his friend, Sammy Scarecrow.

Late one day, the farmer and his wife went out with some friends. All was quiet. Then the sheep began bleating.

'Ted!' a man called. 'Get the sheep into the shed!'

The men got the sheep into the shed and locked the door. Then they went to fetch a truck.

'Sammy!' said Donny. 'We must stop them stealing the sheep!'

Donny pushed Sammy in his bucket towards the shed.

'How are we going to get inside,' panted Donny.

'Kick that loose plank in the shed wall and push me inside,' said Sammy.

The sheep bleated. But when they saw Donny, they were quiet.

'The sheep are quiet!' said Jim. 'We can get them in the truck!'

They went in and saw the tall shape of Sammy Scarecrow! Behind him, Donny brayed and stamped and kicked up dust.

'How did that monster get in?' cried Jim. 'We locked the door!'

'Time we were off!' cried Ted.

Out they ran, shouting and yelling, just as the farmer came home! 'Robbers!' he shouted. 'What has scared them?' He went to see.

'Look!' he said. 'Donny kicked in the loose plank to get inside the shed! But how did Sammy get inside?'

'Donny must have pushed him,' said his wife. 'We always knew that Sammy was his friend!'

READ THESE WORDS AGAIN!

never	friend
quiet	bleating
called	fetch
loose	inside
pushed	panted
monster	shape
scared	robbers

WHAT CAN YOU SEE HERE?

sheep

shed

scarecrow

plank

bucket

WHERE IS THE LOST CHICK?

Hetty Hen was counting her chicks. 'One, two, three, four, five, six! All my chicks are here!'

They went to the yard.

'One, two, three, four, five,' counted Hetty. 'Where is chick number six?'

'We went to the duck pond,' said the first chick. So, off they went.

'I have lost a chick!' said Hetty.

'We shall look for it!' quacked Debbie Duck.

'We went to the farmhouse,' said the second chick.

'To see Kitten!' said the third. So, off they went. Five chicks and the ducks.

'I have lost a chick!' said Hetty.

'I shall look for it!' said Kitten.

'We went to the cowshed,' said the fourth chick. So, off they went. Five chicks, ducks and Kitten.

'I have lost a chick!' said Hetty.

'I shall look for it!' said Cora Cow.

'We went to the stable,' said the fifth chick. So, off they went. Five chicks, ducks, Kitten and Cora.

'I have lost a chick!' said Hetty.

'Let us go to the meadow!' said Hector.

So, off they went. Five chicks, ducks, Kitten, Cora Cow and Hector Horse.

Hetty looked around. 'One, two, three, four, five chicks, ducks, Kitten, Cora Cow, Hector Horse...'

'Cheep!' came a voice. 'Cheep! What about me, Mother Hen?'

'My lost chick!' cried Hetty. 'Where have you been?'

'Following you!' cheeped the cheeky chick. 'I think Follow My Leader is a LOVELY game!'

READ THESE WORDS AGAIN!

counting	lost
quacked	shall
first	off
second	fourth
fifth	voice
what	where
following	leader

WHAT CAN YOU SEE HERE?

duck pond

cow

six chicks

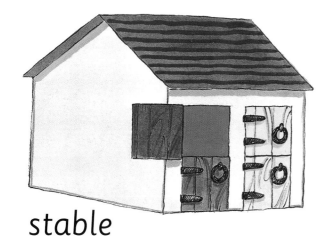

stable

Kitten

THE PUMPKIN PATCH

The farmer's wife was proud of her pumpkin patch! 'My first pumpkins!' she said. 'Just look!'

Dinky Dog and Donny Donkey had watched the pumpkins grow. Now each one was big and round and a lovely orange colour.

'A pumpkin grows so big!' said Dinky.

'Bigger than an onion,' said Donny.

'LOTS bigger than a tomato!' said Dinky.

The bigger the pumpkins grew, the more wasps buzzed around.

'Wasps!' said the farmer's wife. 'I wish I could get rid of them!'

Still the wasps buzzed, until Dinky could stand it no longer.

WHACK! She slapped her paw at a wasp. It buzzed away. SLAP! Donny hit out at a wasp buzzing around a pumpkin. SPLAT! The pumpkin broke. He hit out again. SPLAT! Another pumpkin in bits!

WHACK! Dinky hit out again. SPLAT! Donny trod on a pumpkin! WHACK! Another pumpkin broke, and another. All the pumpkins were soon in pieces!

'What will the farmer's wife say?' said Dinky at last.

'Donny!' came a voice. 'Dinky! What have you done?'

'Well..' Dinky began.

But the farmer's wife held up her hand and smiled.

'You have saved me the job of picking the pumpkins!' she cried. 'And I do not have to cut them up ready to cook! Well done! You shall have some pumpkin pie!'

READ THESE WORDS AGAIN!

wife   patch

watched   orange

colour   bigger

buzzed   longer

broke   another

pieces   saved

picking   ready

WHAT CAN YOU SEE HERE?

pumpkin

onion

wasps

tomato

pie

HECTOR'S EXCITING DAY

Hector once saw a parade of people with flags and policemen on horseback. He thought it was so exciting!

'I shall be in a carnival next week!' a police horse told him.

'How exciting!' said Hector.

'My brother is a racehorse!' said the horse. 'The prizes he has won!'

'How exciting!' said Hector.

'My uncle is in the circus,' said the horse. 'He has been on T.V.'

'How exciting!' said Hector. 'Just one exciting day would suit me!'

'Hector!' cried the farmer. 'Look at your hoof prints on my new path!'

Without thinking, the farmer took a step forward. Too late! His leg got stuck! 'Help!' he cried. 'Help!'

Off Hector galloped to get help. He saw the shepherd and Dinky Dog leading the sheep to the meadow.

'Dinky!' cried Hector. Dinky looked up. The sheep spread out. The shepherd blew his whistle. He wanted Dinky to round the sheep up again.

The sheep rushed forward, nearly knocking Hector over!

Off he galloped into a field. The moment he stopped, he heard the sound of distant music. As he walked on it got louder and louder.

'TWANG! TWANG!' came the sound of a guitar. 'BANG! BANG!' went a drum. 'HURRAH!' cheered a crowd.

There was a pop concert in one of the farmer's fields.

The noise was too much for Hector. He galloped off. The day had been much too exciting for him!

READ THESE WORDS AGAIN!

parade	horseback
exciting	prizes
suit	galloped
forward	shepherd
whistle	knocking
noise	field
crowd	concert

WHAT CAN YOU SEE HERE?

hoof prints

flag

circus

guitar

racehorse

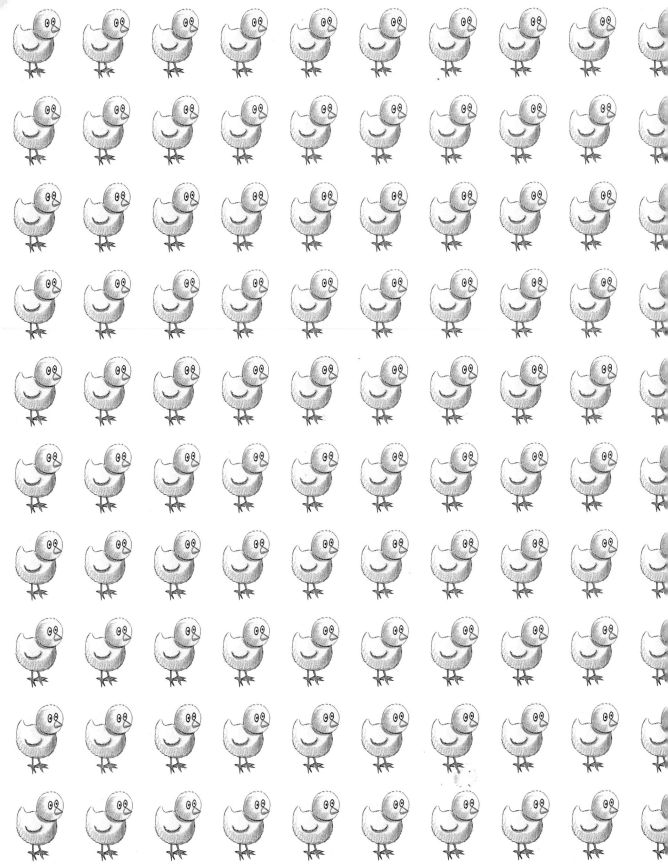